ELEANOR FARJEON (1881–1965) was a British author of children's stories and plays, poetry, biography, history and satire. She lived much of her life among the literary and theatrical circles of London, and her friends included D. H. Lawrence, Walter de la Mare and Robert Frost. One of England's most notable writers for children, Eleanor Farjeon received many honours during her long and distinguished career, including the Regina Medal, the Hans Christian Andersen Award and the Carnegie Medal. The highly prestigious Eleanor Farjeon Award for children's literature is presented annually in her memory by the Children's Book Circle.

Also by Eleanor Farjeon

KINGS AND QUEENS
(*with Herbert Farjeon*)

ELEANOR FARJEON

THE OLD NURSE'S STOCKING-BASKET

Illustrated by Edward Ardizzone

A PUFFIN BOOK

PUFFIN BOOKS

UK | USA | Canada | Ireland | Australia
India | New Zealand | South Africa

Puffin Books is part of the Penguin Random House group of companies
whose addresses can be found at global.penguinrandomhouse.com.

www.penguin.co.uk
www.puffin.co.uk
www.ladybird.co.uk

Penguin
Random House
UK

First published by Oxford University Press 1931
Published by Jonathan Cape 2015
Reissued in this edition 2016

002

Set in 13.5/20.5 pt Sabon LT Std
Typeset by Jouve (UK), Milton Keynes
Printed and bound in Great Britain by Clays Ltd, Elcograf S.p.A.

A CIP catalogue record for this book is available from the British Library

ISBN: 978-0-141-36868-9

All correspondence to:
Puffin Books
Penguin Random House Children's
80 Strand, London WC2R 0RL

Contents

1. The Old Nurse   1
2. Bertha Goldfoot   10
3. The Blue Lotus   25
4. The Proud Infanta   34
5. Can Men Be Such Fools As All That?   43
6. The Veil of Irazade   52
7. Lipp the Lapp   59
8. The Roof-tree   61
9. You Can't Darn *That* Hole   69
10. The Princess of China   78
11. The Golden Eagle   88
12. The Two Brothers   97
13. The Sea-Baby   104

Contents

1. The Old Nurse

THE OLD Nurse was putting the children to bed by the fire. The night nursery was such a big one that each of the four children had a bed to itself, and still there was plenty of room to play and hide in. The fire in the big old-fashioned fireplace threw a dancing red light into the many corners made by the shape of the room itself, and also by the tall dark wooden chests and presses against the walls, and by the queer sloping ceiling, which in some places almost touched the floor. For the night nursery was really a great attic at the top of the house in which the children lived.

The names of the children were Doris, Ronald, Roland and Mary Matilda. Mary Matilda was the baby, and she was three and a half. Ronald and Roland were twins, and they were five – they looked so much alike that you could hardly tell which was which, till you discovered that Ronald had a tiny brown mole tucked into the left side of his nose, while Roland's mole (for he had to have one too) was tucked into his right nostril. Even then you couldn't always remember whether it was Ronald whose mole was on the left and Roland's on the right, or the other way round. Their very names were so much alike that it was a bother; till people fell into the way of calling them Ronnie and Roley, which made a little more difference. As for Doris, she was the eldest, and felt very old indeed, because she was seven. But even so, she wasn't nearly or *nearly* as old as the Old Nurse.

Nobody knew how old the Old Nurse was. She had been their nurse ever since Doris could remember. And before that, she had been Mother's nurse, ever since *she* could remember. And when Granny came to see them (and she was a *very* old lady, with her hair turning grey), she would say to the Old Nurse,

'Well, Nanny, how are you feeling today?'

And the Old Nurse would answer, 'As spry as a kitten, my dear. And I hope you've been behaving yourself, though I dare say you haven't since I stopped keeping my eye on you! Ah, you were one of my bad children, you were!'

The first time Doris heard the Old Nurse say this, she asked in surprise, 'Were you Granny's nurse, too, Nanny?'

'Dear, dear, wasn't I!' said the Old Nurse. 'And a rare handful she was. But she hasn't turned out so bad, after all, though one never knows, even yet. I dare say she'll do, in the long run. For I gave her a good start.'

'What sort of a start, Nanny?' asked Ronnie. 'Did you jump out at her from behind the door and say *Boo*?'

'Oh, you stupid!' cried Doris. 'Nanny doesn't mean *that* kind of a start at all. She means she brought Granny up nicely to be a good little girl, like she's bringing up me and you.'

'I'm *not* stupid,' said Ronnie, frowning, 'and I *won't* be brought up like a good little girl.'

'Stupid!' said Doris again. 'You know what I mean.'

'I know what you *said*,' snapped Ronnie. 'And *you're* stupid.'

'Children,' said the Old Nurse, 'stop quarrelling, or you know what.'

The children did know what, and when the Old Nurse said this, they nearly always stopped quarrelling at once. For it meant that there would be no story that night, after they were in bed. And the Old Nurse's stories were one of the best bits of the day, when they were sitting or lying under the cool sheets and snug blankets, munching their supper-biscuits, and drinking their milk, before they brushed their teeth, last thing of all, and the Old Nurse turned out the gas.

There was no end to the Old Nurse's stories; her memory went back such a long way that she never need tell the same tale twice, only sometimes they asked her to, if they remembered a special favourite. And she might answer, 'Yes, I'll tell you that tale tonight, for it's just the size of the hole in this stocking,' or she might say, 'No, that tale is too big, and the hole in this stocking is too little; they won't fit. I must tell you something else.'

For you must know that while the children had their supper, the Old Nurse did a bit of darning; her stocking-basket was always full of the four children's stockings, with holes in the toes and heels, and even in the knees. And the Old Nurse would fish out a pair by chance, and draw it down over her left hand, and turn it this way and that, looking for the hole. And then, while she threaded her darning needle with the right worsted, she would fish about in her memory for a tale to fit the hole, and when the hole was finished, the tale was done. The children always watched anxiously when she was looking at the stocking for the hole in it, because a little hole only meant a little story, and a big hole meant a longer story. Sometimes Ronnie and Roley would fall down on the gravel on purpose, and scrape up a hole in the stocking-knee that would be sure to mean a long story when the Old Nurse came to darn it. But Doris, who was rather a good little girl, never did this; her stocking-holes were mostly in the toes and heels, where her shoes had rubbed them or her toenails were too long. As for Mary Matilda, the tiny holes in her socks meant very little stories indeed. So Roley would sometimes sneak her socks out of the stocking-basket, and hide them before bedtime.

On this particular night, when the children were in bed, the Old Nurse rummaged as usual in the basket, and drew out one of Doris's long brown stockings, and found quite a nice-sized hole in the heel of it; and as she flattened the worsted tight round the darning needle, before passing it through the long eye, she said thoughtfully, 'Well, well, that's just the size of the hole little Bertha Goldfoot always made in her heel when I was her nurse in Germany.'

'How long ago, Nanny?' asked Doris.

'Let me think, now,' said the Old Nurse. 'Was it a hundred years ago, or two? I know it was long before I nursed the Brothers Grimm, because they were always teasing me to tell them the tale, when *they* were little boys, but for some reason I never told them that one. I expect they'd been too naughty or something, so it never got put down in their

book later on. They were nice boys but I had to spank 'em sometimes.'

'But what about Bertha Goldfoot, Nanny?' asked Doris again, for when the Old Nurse went rambling on like that you sometimes missed the story altogether.

'Oh, Bertha. Well, I dare say it happened about five hundred years ago – or seven. One can't be too particular. Now be quiet, children, while I get this hole started.'

2. Bertha Goldfoot

I HAD been nurse to Bertha Goldfoot's father when he was a little boy, and after he grew up and was married, I stayed on in his castle until Bertha was born, and then I became *her* nurse. Bertha's father was a baron. He had a castle on the banks of the Rhine, or rather, on a rock above the bank; and under his castle on the edge of the water nestled the little village that paid him tribute, where the villagers led happy lives in their little houses with pointed red roofs, and in the vineyards on the hills between the village and the castle.

For their baron was a fairly kind baron, which all the German barons in those times and parts were not. But then, I couldn't have the upbringing of *all* of them. It was the custom for every villager to bring the Baron a gold piece a year; and even in the hard years he could not let them off, because he himself had to pay tribute to the King. If he failed to do so the King might come down on him and seize his castle, and lands, and everything he had. And the villagers themselves would not have been so well off under anyone else as under their own baron; so they were as anxious as he was to keep the King in a good temper. Nobody had ever seen the King in those parts, but it was whispered that he only cared for money and dancing, and if he were denied them could show a very bad temper when he liked. Like some little boys I know (said the Old Nurse, darting a sudden look at Ronnie and Roley).

When Bertha was born, there was a christening, of course, and all the noblemen and noblewomen of the countryside came to it, and also, of course, all the chief fairies. The Baron and his wife tried to remember every fairy of importance, for they knew something bad might happen to their child if one was forgotten. They even invited the Lorelei, the lovely water nymph who sits and sings on a rock in the middle of the Rhine, and with her magic song draws men to their death. Many a friend of the Baron had been drowned at the foot of the Lorelei's rock, but the Baron did not dare leave her out, all the same. She did not appear, however, until the feast was over, and everybody had presented his gift and departed. Then, as the Baron and his wife and I were alone with little Bertha in her cradle, the doors of the great hall swung open, and the lovely Lorelei glided in, with her mantle of gold hair flowing about her like the golden waters of the Rhine. And like the river, it was wet, and so were her green garments, and her white skin. She stepped up to the cradle, and leaning over touched the baby's right foot with her wet finger, saying, 'Child, men shall call you Bertha Goldfoot. The Lorelei gives you a foot of gold from the day you are able to walk.'

Then she glided out of the hall, leaving a trail of water on the floor behind her. And none of us knew what she meant by her gift. While we were wondering, we heard a horrid little chuckle, and up through the floor popped Rumpelstiltskin, the Stocking Elf. Everyone knows what a nasty little

creature *he* is, and the Baron had not even thought of inviting him to the christening, because he is not of any great importance in the fairy world. Even if he was offended, it was not in his power to do much harm, but we all felt uneasy as he hopped over to the cradle, and pointed his finger at Bertha's left foot.

'Child,' he croaked, 'you shall always have a hole in your left stocking as long as you live. That's what Rumpelstiltskin gives you for a christening gift!'

With that he disappeared as suddenly as he had come. The Baron said, 'It's bad enough, but it might have been much worse,' but I myself wasn't so sure, for it's the little things that matter most. And the Baron's wife said, 'For my part, I think the Lorelei's gift was the worse of the two. If the child grows up with a gold foot, how shall we ever get her married? Nobody would want a wife with such an oddity about her.'

'We must keep her foot covered up all the time, so that nobody shall guess,' said the Baron. 'See to it for us, Nanny,' he added, turning to me. 'Luckily the guests have all gone, and the three of us can keep Bertha's gold foot a secret between us until she is married.'

The first year of the baby's life, I spent all my spare time in knitting stockings for her, against the day when she would be able to walk; for it was then that she was to get her gold foot. The first time I saw her totter on to her little feet, to try to run from me to her mother, I caught the child up, and pulled on her stockings, so that the whole of her feet and ankles were covered; for if a maid or a page had happened to catch a glimpse of the golden foot, the story would travel through the land. Then we let little Bertha begin to toddle as she pleased; but from that day she wore no more socks, because socks can slip down to the ankle – as Mary Matilda knows!

Bertha even had to sleep in her stockings; and I was careful always to change them at night in the dark, so that even I never saw her right foot after she was one year old. Her left foot, on the other hand, everybody saw; at least, they saw a part of it. For almost as soon as her left stocking was on, a big hole came in the heel like magic. It was no use scolding her, or watching to see how it happened – there the hole was! At first I would change the stocking at once, but five minutes later I had to change it again, and at last I said to the Baron and his wife, 'It's no manner of good, my dears. We can't keep the holes from coming, so the child will have to wear boots.' And from the time she was about two, Bertha did. It wasn't very pleasant for her to have to wear boots from morning to night, no matter what she was doing, but it couldn't be helped. Boots she wore, from her babyhood to her eighteenth birthday, when she was as beautiful a young woman as any baron's daughter on the Rhine. Moreover, everybody loved her, from her parents to the barefoot boat-boy in the village, with whom she had often played in her childhood. As she grew older, suitors for her hand began to present themselves, but she cared for none of them.

Now this year was, as it happened, a terribly bad one for the vine harvest. The blight had got into it somehow; the grapes rotted, and the peasants in the village were as poor as church mice in consequence. At the end of the season they came weeping to the castle door and asked audience of the Baron.

'My lord,' said the Chief Vine-grower, 'our hearts are broken and our pockets too. We cannot pay you the tribute this year.'

'If you do not,' said the Baron, 'both you and I will be ruined. For the bad year has hit me as well as you, and if I do not pay him the King will descend on us in wrath.'

'My lord,' said the peasants, 'our children are starving, and we have nothing left. We would pay you gladly if we could; but who can pay what he has not got?'

The Baron was very angry, for he was not always a reasonable man; and kind as he really was, he was prepared to punish them, when Bertha, who was sitting at his feet, looked up at him, saying, 'They cannot help it, Father. Let us hope for the best, and heaven will soften the King's heart or will send us the means to pay him.'

Her smile was so sweet that the Baron could not resist it, and he said to the peasants, 'Well, then, whatever bad fortune may fall upon us, we will share it together.' And the peasants returned to the village, thanking him and blessing his daughter.

But heaven did not soften the King's heart. He came riding in wrath, with his soldiers behind him, to demand the reason why the Baron had not paid him the tribute. The Baron pointed out to him the blighted vines, saying, 'There, sire, lies all my fortune, in ruins. The grapes were my gold, and gave me the gold I gave you.'

'And gold I will have!' said the King. 'I care not for your reasons. If you cannot pay me, I will take your castle, your village and all you possess.'

As he spoke, Bertha came into the hall. Her mother and I had dressed her in a gown of white silk, and crowned her head with her golden plaits, hoping that her beauty might win the King's heart, and save the day. Indeed, he stood amazed with admiration, as I knew he would, and turning to the Baron said, 'Who is this maiden?'

'My daughter, sire,' he answered.

'In that case, Baron,' said the King, 'I will marry your daughter, and her wedding portion shall be the debt you owe me.'

I could see that the Baron was overjoyed, and so was his wife. Bertha, poor child, turned as pale as her gown, and cast down her eyes before the King, who was admiring her from top to toe. But when his gaze *did* reach her toes, he frowned a little, and asked, 'Why does she wear boots?'

The Baron stammered hastily, 'She has been out walking, and has only just come in.'

'Put on your shoes,' said the King to Bertha, 'for I would like to see how my bride can dance.'

'I have no shoes, Your Majesty,' said Bertha; and this was true – she had never had a pair of shoes since she was a baby.

'Then I will dance with you in your stocking feet,' said the King. And it was no use protesting. Bertha had to take off her boots before him, and there, in the heel of her left stocking, was an enormous hole. The King looked surprised, and bade her go and change her stockings. But what was the use? She came back with a hole as big as before. A third time she tried, and still her rosy left heel was bare to everybody's view, and her cheeks were rosier still, as she hung her head and blushed for shame.

The King's admiration now turned to scorn, and he said to the Baron, 'Beautiful as your daughter is, I cannot have a slattern for my queen. Farewell; but if the money is not paid by tomorrow, I will turn you out of your castle.' So saying, he rode away.

The Baron now turned in anger on his daughter. 'It is you, with your wretched gift, who have brought me to this!' he cried. 'You are not fit to be my daughter, you slattern! Go away from my castle for ever, but go barefoot. It is better for the world to see your gold foot at last, than to see you with a hole in your stocking.'

He himself pulled off her stockings; and when he uncovered her right foot, lo and behold! it was as white as her left. It surprised us all, for if Bertha's foot was not gold, what did the Lorelei mean by the gift? But the Baron was in too much of a rage to care about this; he lifted her in his arms and bore her

down to the village, crying, 'My peasants, thanks to my daughter, I am now a beggar like yourselves. Who wants a beggar's daughter for his wife?'

While the people stood round amazed, the barefooted boat-boy, whom Bertha had played with as a child, stepped forward and said modestly, 'I want her, my lord, if she will have me.' And Bertha nodded her golden head, and the Baron, with a harsh laugh, gave her into the boy's arms and strode away. The boy called to the priest to ring the wedding bell at once, and set Bertha down on the ground; and for the first time since she was a year old, Bertha's bare foot touched the earth, and they walked to church together. But here is the strange thing. Wherever her right foot stepped, it left behind it a piece of gold. So that the whole of her way into church and out again was marked by a double line of shining coins. And the people following after cried in astonishment, 'Bertha Goldfoot! Look, there goes Bertha Goldfoot!' So it was for the rest of the day; the fiddler and piper struck up for the wedding dance, and the people danced in their shoes, with the barefoot bride and groom in their midst. And wherever Bertha danced, the gold danced under her very toes. By midnight there was so much gold on the ground that the peasants were kept busy sweeping it up; and in the morning they carried it in a sack to the Baron and said, 'Here is our tribute, my lord. The village is saved.'

The Baron was now as joyful as he had been angry; he sent the gold post-haste to the King, and asked how it had all come about. And when he heard that it was due to the wonderful gift of his own daughter, he hastened down to the village and forgave her.

'Come back to the castle with me, my darling child!' he said.

But Bertha shook her golden head and laughed. 'I cannot, Father. I am married now, and must live with my husband. Besides,' said she, 'I can never wear stockings again, for my gold foot loses its power unless it goes bare. But neither you nor the peasants need fear poverty any more.'

Her father embraced her, and saw that it must be so. And from then to the end of her days, Bertha and her husband, and all their children, too, lived barefoot – so *she* had no stockings to darn (said the Old Nurse).

3. The Blue Lotus

RONNIE had been naughty. He knew he had and he went to bed crying, while the other children went to bed the same as usual, without taking very much notice. For they were sometimes naughty too, and they knew that when you've been naughty you've just got to get over it. The Old Nurse sat darning away by the fire, and did not try to tell a story yet; but she kept an ear on Ronnie, and first his crying sounded angry, and the Old Nurse said to herself, 'Ah, *those* tears won't wash very much away!' But presently the angry sound changed to a sorry sound, and then the Old Nurse said to herself, 'It will soon be washed away now.' As Ronnie's crying grew less, she heard him get out of bed and go across the room, and get into Roley's bed; for it was Roley to whom he had been naughty. The Old Nurse looked round and said, 'There's a tight fit! Do you think you can manage to have your suppers side by side? Don't get your knees mixed up, and don't knock your elbows into each other, and don't make too many crumbs in the sheets.' She brought Ronnie's supper over to him, and got a big sponge, and washed his face, saying, 'I haven't washed off so many tear stains since I washed the Prince of India's face by the Lotus Lake.'

'When, Nanny?' asked Roley; while Ronnie asked, 'Did the Prince of India have *many* more tears than me?'

'Yes, he did, and needed them too! Let me see when it was. It was before I was nurse to the Inca of Peru, but after I was nurse to the Sphinx of Egypt – or else it was the other way round. A body can't remember. Anyhow, it was a very long time ago.'

The Prince of India began by being the very worst boy I ever nursed in my life. He cried about everything, and got into fearful tempers; and even his gentle mother, the Ranee, could do nothing with him, much as she loved him, and much as he loved her. In between his fits of temper he was quite a nice boy, though, and one day he asked his mother, 'Why do I cry so much?'

'I don't know,' she said. 'Perhaps it is your heart makes you cry, when you have been in a temper.'

'Then I won't have a heart!' said the Prince of India.

'Oh,' begged his mother, 'don't say that! It would be better not to have a temper than not to have a heart.'

'No, it wouldn't,' said the little Prince haughtily. 'I *like* my temper, and I don't like my heart.'

So he sent for his Magician and told him to take away his heart. The poor Ranee, his mother, said to the Magician, 'You must not do this – I forbid it.' And at once the Prince flew into another of his tempers and said to his Magician, 'Turn my mother into a White Elephant!' And as the Prince was greater in the land even than his mother, the Magician had to obey him. He turned the Ranee into a

White Elephant, and took away the Prince's heart; so the Prince had not time to be sorry for what he had done, and he let the White Elephant go sadly out of the palace into the jungle, and didn't care a bit.

Then he said to the Magician, 'You mustn't hurt my heart, or I would die; but you must put it somewhere quite safe, where I can't get at it, and nobody will know where it is.'

The Magician bowed three times, and went away with the Prince of India's heart. He carried it to a pool in the middle of the jungle, and laid the heart inside a blue lotus-flower that grew in the middle of the pool. Then he cast a magic spell on the water of the pool, so that whoever touched a drop of its water would die; and so the Prince's heart was kept safe from the hands of men. The only one who heard the spell was the White Elephant, who had followed the Magician to see what he would do with the heart of her son. And every morning and evening she came down to the pool and plucked with her long trunk a forest-flower whose cup was full of dew. Then she stretched her trunk over the pool, and tilted the cup so that the sweet dew fell on the Prince's heart, and kept it refreshed.

Meanwhile a year went by, and the Prince's temper grew worse than ever; and all the worse because now he never cried. He only stormed and raged when he wanted anything he could not have. So in the end he had everything he wanted, and then he wanted something else.

One day he said he would go tiger hunting in the jungle, so a great party was made, with the Prince riding on one elephant, and me on another, and other people on horses, and still others on foot. But there seemed to be no tigers in the jungle that day, and we went on and on till we came in the evening to the pool, which the Prince had never seen before. As soon as he set eyes on the beautiful Blue Lotus

standing up on its tall stem in the water, he forgot all about tigers and cried, 'Oh, what a lovely flower! I want it.'

And he jumped down off his elephant and rushed to the edge of the pool.

Just at that moment, the White Elephant also approached the pool, with the flower-cup of dew in her trunk. She alone knew that the water of the pool was poisoned, and that if her son touched it he would die. Casting away the flower, she quickly stretched her trunk across the pool, plucked the Blue Lotus off its stem and laid it at her son's feet without wetting it by a single drop. But alas! though the Lotus had escaped the touch of the water, her trunk had not; and no sooner had she dropped the Lotus into the Prince's hands, than the White Elephant lay down and died.

The Prince picked up the Lotus with his heart in it, as fresh as it had been when he was born, and as he held it, looking down on the White Elephant whom he knew to be his mother, he began to weep for the first time in a year. He wept and wept and wept – you could not have counted his tears if you had tried for a month. He wept all over his mother's body, and as his tears fell upon it, the tough white hide began to shrivel, like old leaves wasted by the rain. And at the end of an hour it was all washed away, and the Ranee, his mother, stepped out, living, as lovely as ever. And she and the Prince did not stop hugging each other for another hour.

Then the Prince called his Magician and said, 'Put back my heart and take away my temper.' So the Magician did, and he dropped the Prince's temper to the bottom of the pool, where nobody could get at it any more. And then I got off my elephant, and wiped the tear-stains off the Prince of India's face; and it took me just as long to get it clean as it has taken me to tell you this story.

4. The Proud Infanta

'OH, NANNY,' said Doris, as the Old Nurse pulled one of her long pale-pink stockings out of the basket, 'please don't darn that one!'

'Why not, my dear?' asked the Old Nurse. 'It needs darning very badly. There's a wide ladder all down the front of the leg.'

'Yes, Nanny, I know there is, just where it will show and look horrid. Do throw it away.'

'But it's your very Sunday-best silk party stocking, dear. What will you do at the next party if you've only one stocking to wear?'

Doris pouted. 'I'd rather not go to the party than wear *that* stocking. Everybody would look, and I'd feel horrid.'

'Now, my dear, don't you go getting proud,' said the Old Nurse, threading a very fine needle with very fine silk. 'Pride is one of the worst spoil sports in the world, nearly as bad as envy, but not quite. If you're going through life ashamed to wear a darned stocking, I'll say you are no better than the Infanta of Spain I once was nurse to, who was proud of all the wrong things and ashamed of all the right ones.'

'What was she proud of, Nanny?' asked Doris.

'Well, that's just what I used to say,' said the Old Nurse, 'when she got so proud that there was no bearing with her. She was too proud to say thank you to the footman who picked up her handkerchief for her, and too proud to eat her dinner off a silver plate instead of a golden one, and too proud to have her coach drawn by anything but a milk-white horse with blue eyes, a silver bridle and an azure plume, and a jet horse with scarlet eyes, a golden bridle and a scarlet plume. If there was one white hair in the black horse's tail, or one black hair in the white horse's mane, she had them banished out of Spain.'

'What are you so proud of?' I asked her time and again.

'I wonder you can ask, Nanny,' she would answer haughtily. 'Am I not the Infanta of Spain? Have I not the widest golden dress sewn with the costliest pearls in Europe? Must not everybody bow to me as I pass by? Will not the greatest kings in the world beg one day to marry me? Has not my father more money in his chests, and more lands in foreign parts, and more ships on the sea, than any other ruler upon earth? And will not all these be mine one day? I wonder at you, for asking why I am proud.'

'Well, well, so do I!' I told my young lady. 'For I see you can't help it.'

That afternoon we went for a ride in the Infanta's gold coach, drawn by the jet and ivory horses. A little way out of the town we came to a small village, and outside the village bakers' we saw a peasant woman sitting with her naked baby on her knee, a chubby, laughing baby, as brown as a berry. The mother was dancing him up and down, singing to him,

'Oh dear me, how proud I feel!
I'm the proudest woman in all Castile!
I can bake the best loaf from the miller's corn,
And I've got the best baby that ever was born!'

The Infanta leaned out of the window to listen to the song, and when it was done her eyes flashed with anger. She jumped out of the coach, and ran up to the woman and said, 'That song of yours is full of lies. *I* am the proudest one in all Castile. I am the Infanta of Spain, and that is something that nobody else can be. But *any*body can bake a loaf and have a baby.'

The happy peasant laughed gaily, showing her beautiful white teeth. 'Ah, little lady,' she cried, 'but not the best loaf, and not the best baby. Can they, my pet?' And she buried her face in her baby's fat neck, and filled the creases with kisses.

'Yes, they can!' cried the proud Infanta. And she jumped back into the coach, told the coachman to drive home to the palace, went straight to the kitchen, and demanded flour and a basin of the astonished cook. When she had got them, she poured some water on the flour and pressed it together into a big hard

ball with her angry little hands, and told the
cook to put it in the oven till it was done, and
then to send it up for her father's supper. When
it came to table, you never saw such a loaf! It
was as hard as a stone.

'What's this, what's this?' asked the King of
Spain.

'It's a loaf for your supper, Father,' said the
little Infanta proudly. 'I made it myself with
my own hands.'

The King tried to cut it with a knife,
and then with his sword; then he burst out
laughing and said to the Head Carver, 'Send
this to the Commander-in-Chief with the

King's compliments, and tell him to use it for a cannonball when next he fights the Moors.'

The Infanta got as red as a turkey-cock; she left the table and the room with her chin in the air, and refused all supper and comfort. The next morning she said she would go for a drive all by herself; I could see she was still much upset, and wanted to go with her, but she would not let me. Every day for a month she went out by herself in her grand coach, and told nobody where she went to; and when we asked the coachman, he said she had given him orders to hold his tongue.

Then one night at suppertime, as the King and the Infanta sat together at table, another loaf was brought in on a golden salver, as before; and it smelled so hot and crusty, and looked such a beautiful golden brown, that the King instantly cut a big slice, and ate it without butter. When he had eaten it, he exclaimed, 'What bread! What delicious bread! I've never tasted such a good loaf in all my life.'

And the Infanta of Spain once more got as red as a turkey-cock, but this time with pleasure, as she said, 'I made it myself, Father, with my own two hands. It is not yet quite as good as the loaf the baker's wife in the village bakes, but she says that one day she wouldn't wonder if I baked even better than she does.'

The King of Spain opened his arms to his daughter, and said, 'I am proud of a daughter who can bake such a loaf!'

And the Infanta went and took his kiss, looking prouder than I have ever seen her look before.

But I saw her look still prouder, years after, when she sent for me to come and be nurse to her first baby. She had married the King of France, and I had not seen her since her wedding day. She came herself to meet me at the palace door, and when I had embraced her

I asked, 'Well, and what is the baby like, my dear?'

'Oh, Nanny!' she said joyously. 'I'm the proudest woman in the world. I've got the best baby that ever was born. *That's* something to be proud of, isn't it?'

5. Can Men Be Such Fools As All That?

'LOOK at that now!' said the Old Nurse, holding up a pair of thick grey stockings that looked less like stockings than a bunch of rags. 'It isn't even a hole – it's nothing but tatters. Aren't you ashamed of yourself, Roley?'

'Those aren't Roley's stockings, they're mine,' said Ronnie. 'I did it getting through a wire fence.'

'And whose stockings are these, then?' asked the Old Nurse, holding up another thick grey pair, just as ragged as the others.

'Oh, those are mine,' said Roley. 'I did it when I got through the fence after Ronnie.'

The Old Nurse shook her head. 'There's no telling you boys apart; whether by your faces, your stockings or the things you do,' she said. 'You are almost as much alike as the little Duke of Chinon and the Rag-picker's Son.'

'Who were they?' asked Ronnie. 'Were you the Rag-picker's Son's nurse, Nanny?'

'No,' said the Old Nurse, 'the Rag-picker was so poor that his son had to bring himself up; which he did quite happily, with old clothes to wear, bread and garlic to eat, and a little mongrel dog called Jacques to play with on the banks of the River Loire.'

But I was nurse to the little Duke of Chinon, who lived in the great grim castle on the hill above the town where the Rag-picker's Son lived. The little Duke, of course, had everything that the poor boy hadn't: fine clothes to wear, white bread and chicken to eat, and a pedigree spaniel called Hubert for a playfellow.

Except for all these differences, the two boys were as like as two peas; when I took the little Duke walking by the river, and we happened to meet the Rag-picker's Son, you could not have told one from the other, if one hadn't worn satin and the other rags, while one had a dirty face and hands and the other was as clean as a new pin. Everybody remarked on it.

The little Duke used to look longingly at the poor boy, though, for he was allowed to splash about in the water of the river as he pleased; and the water of the Loire is more beautiful to splash about in than any water in France, for it is as clear as honey, and has the brightest gold sand bed you can imagine; and when you get out of the town, it runs between sandy shores, where green willows grow, and flowers of all sorts. But it was against my orders to let the little Duke play in the water,

and I had to obey them, though I was sorry
for him; for I knew what boys like.

One day as we were out walking, the Duke's
spaniel Hubert ran up to the Rag-picker's
Son's mongrel, Jacques, and they touched
noses and made friends. And the Duke and
the poor boy smiled at each other and said,
'Hullo!' After that, when we met, the boys
always nodded, or winked, or made some sign
of friendship; and one day the Rag-picker's
Son jerked his thumb at the river, as much as

to say, 'Come in and play with me!' The Duke looked at me, and I shook my head, so the Duke shook his. But he was cross with me for the rest of the day.

The next day I missed him, and there was a great hullabaloo all over the castle. I and his guardian and all his attendants went down to the town to find him, and asked everybody we met if they had seen him; and presently we met the Rag-picker, who said, 'Yes, I saw him an hour ago, going along the river bank with my son.' And we all ran along the bank, the Rag-picker too, and most of the townsfolk behind us.

A mile along the bank, there they were, the two boys, standing in the middle of the river as bare as when they were born, splashing about and screaming with laughter; and on the shore lay a little heap of clothes, rags and fine linen all thrown down anyhow together. We were all very angry with the boys, and called and shouted to them to come out of

the water; and they shouted back that they wouldn't. At last the Rag-picker waded in and fetched them out by the scruffs of their necks. And there they stood before us, naked and grinning and full of fun, and just as the Duke's guardian was going to scold his charge, and the Rag-picker to scold his son, they suddenly found themselves in a pickle! For without their clothes, washed clean by the river, they were so exactly alike, that we didn't know which was which. And the boys saw that we didn't, and grinned more than ever.

'Now then, my boy!' said the Rag-picker to one of them. But the boy he spoke to did not answer, for he knew if he talked it would give the game away.

And the Duke's guardian said to the other boy, 'Come, monseigneur!' But that boy too shook his head and kept mum.

Then I had a bright idea, and said to the boys, 'Put on your clothes!' for I thought that would settle it. But the two boys picked up the clothes as they came: one of them put on the ragged shirt and the satin coat, and the other put on the fine shirt and the ragged coat. So we were no better off than before.

Then the Rag-picker and the Duke's guardian lost their tempers, and raised their sticks and gave each of the boys three strokes, thinking that might help; but all it did was to make them squeal, and when a boy squeals it doesn't matter if he's a Duke or a beggar, the sound is just the same.

'This is dreadful,' said the Duke's guardian: 'for all we know, we shall get the boys mixed for ever, and I shall take the Rag-picker's Son back to the castle, and the Duke will grow up as the Rag-picker's Son. Is there *no* way of telling which is which? Can we all be such fools as that?'

Just as we were scratching our heads and cudgelling our brains, and wondering what on earth to do next, there came a sound of yelps and barks; and out of the willows ran Jacques and Hubert, who had been off on their own, playing together. They came racing towards us joyously, and straight as a die Jacques jumped up and licked the face of the boy in the satin coat, while Hubert licked the boy in the ragged jacket.

So then there was no doubt about it. We made the boys change their coats, and the Rag-picker marched his son home to bed, and the guardian did the same with the Duke. And that night the Duke and the poor boy had exactly the same supper to go to sleep on; in other words, nothing and plenty of it.

But how had the dogs known in the twink of an eye what we hadn't known at all? Can men be such fools as all that?

6. The Veil of Irazade

'WHO WAS the strongest baby you ever nursed, Nanny?' asked Roley, as the Old Nurse fished about in her basket for a stocking with a sensible hole in it. 'Was it me?' For Roley was beginning to be rather pleased with himself, because he could do dumb-bell exercises with heavier dumb-bells than Ronnie.

'Oh dear, no,' said the Old Nurse, 'it wasn't you, and not nearly you. I think it was that boy called Hercules, though it might have been that other one called Samson. They were both strong babies, and I was proud to show 'em off to people when they called.'

'And who was the most beautiful baby?' asked Doris. (Doris did not like to add, like Roley, 'Was it me?' but she had sometimes heard people say, 'What a pretty little girl!' so she rather hoped Nanny might say it was her.)

'Ah, there's no doubt at all about that!' said the Old Nurse, starting on a stocking.

The most beautiful baby I ever nursed was the Princess Irazade of Persia. They may talk as much as they like of the beauty of Queen Helen of Troy, but the Princess Irazade was more beautiful than all the queens of the world rolled into one. She was so beautiful, that it was hardly safe to look at her. From the time she was a baby, she was followed wherever she went; the servants would lie on the stairs in wait for her to come up or down, so that they might catch the tiniest glimpse of her. Her father neglected the business of his kingdom, to stand and gaze at her by the hour together. When Irazade passed through the streets, the whole city followed her until she reached the palace again. When she sat among the tulips in her father's garden, all the birds of the air flew down to see.

As she grew older, there was not a prince or a king on the face of the earth who did not offer himself as a husband for her. None of them had seen her, but the story of her beauty had spread through the world. Men spoke of it, birds sang of it, the winds of heaven breathed it, and the seas murmured it on every shore. Travelling from the two hemispheres, the kings and princes assembled together on a certain day in her father's palace in Persia, and she was brought among them to choose which pleased her best. Her beauty made all hearts stand still as she stood there, gazing round upon her suitors. But it raised such jealousy among the kings, that no sooner had her glance fallen upon one than his neighbour

turned and slew him, lest he should find favour
with the beautiful Irazade. And in the end the
hall was filled with the dead, for the last two
killed each other.

But even this made no difference. There was
now a new king in every country in the world,
and every one of these too proposed to wed
the Persian Princess. We were all much
troubled about it, 'For,' said the King of Persia,
'the same thing will happen again. Nobody
can look upon Irazade without desiring her so
much that his desires will turn him mad.'

At last we decided that for the safety of the world her beauty must be veiled for ever, even from her husband; her beauty was for everyone, or for none. We put a veil over Irazade's face; and when next the kings came to woo her, she was brought among them so that no man could see her face.

'Here is my daughter,' said the King of Persia, 'and the man who weds her must swear never to look upon her, or to let any other look upon her, all the days of her life. Who now among you wants to marry her?'

Then one king and another looked at the veiled figure, and they began to murmur among themselves. They did not like the King of Persia's condition, and they began to doubt the veiled figure of the Princess.

'Who knows if it is the Princess Irazade herself?' said one. 'How easy it would be to pass off upon us some other woman under the veil.'

'And even if it is the Princess Irazade,' said another, 'how do we know that the tale of her beauty is true? Perhaps under the veil she is as ugly as a witch.'

'And even if she is the Princess, and is as beautiful as people say,' said a third, 'what husband wishes to be denied the joy of his wife's beauty? Who would wed a wife under a veil?'

So one and another spoke and went away. At last the hall was empty, and when the King of Persia's condition became known no one ever came again to ask the hand of the beautiful Irazade of Persia.

Time passed; the King and Queen of Persia died, and there was another ruler in the land;

and the old families died out, and others took their places. But in her room in the palace Irazade lived on, unseen by anyone but me. She was so beautiful that she could not die; and I alone knew that the figure under the veil never lost its youth or its loveliness. They thought that Irazade must by now be an old woman, and the story of her beauty became a legend.

At last Persia was conquered by another country; the conqueror drove all the Persians out of the palace, and when they went, the veiled Princess went too. But where she went to no one knows. Only I know, that because such beauty cannot die, she is still wandering somewhere in the world under a veil.

7. Lipp the Lapp

'AND WHO was the littlest baby you ever nursed, Nanny?' asked Doris. 'Was it the Princess of China?'

'No,' said the Old Nurse, examining one of Mary Matilda's tiny socks for a hole. 'No, it wasn't the Princess of China. Little though she was, Lipp was littler still.'

'Who was Lipp?' asked Ronnie.

'Lipp was a Lapp, and was born in Lapland. At least, I heard he was. I was sent for in a great hurry one day, because they said that a baby had been born in Lapland who was so little that his mother couldn't find him. And would I come quick, and see what I could do? So I did. But *I* never found him either.'

'Then what happened?' asked Roley.

'Nothing.'

'But what is the story about Lipp?'

'There isn't a story about Lipp. And if you ask me,' said the Old Nurse mysteriously, 'I don't believe there was any Lipp at all. Any more than there's any hole at all in Mary Matilda's sock. How it got into my basket *I* can't think!'

8. The Roof-Tree

'HERE'S a hole in a little girl's sole,' said the Old Nurse as she dipped into her basket and came up with one of Doris's stockings. 'So tonight I'll tell you a tale about a little girl whose stockings I not only darned, but knitted, when I was her nurse in Switzerland.'

Her name was Liesel, and she was the Forester's daughter. Her father lived on the mountainside, in a beautiful chalet just outside a great forest of pines and fir trees. The forest lay against the mountain, as black as a bearskin spread on a marble floor; and high above the treetops the peaks of the snow-mountains glittered white against the sky when it was sunny, or grew dark when it was stormy, or rosy when the sun went down, or golden when it came up. And when the mists drew round them, the mountains disappeared altogether.

But Liesel was as much at home in the forest among the mountains as you are in your own garden. She had no brothers or sisters, and she made playfellows of all the things that grew in the forest. One of the tallest trees she named after her father, the Forester, and one of the little baby fir trees she named after herself. She would run out at least once a day to have a chat with it, and see how it was getting on, and once, as she and I were going home, she pulled the pink ribbon off one of her two plaits and said, 'I've got two bows, and Liesel's tree has none. I'll give her one of mine.' And laughing, she tied the pink bow on the very tip-top branch.

The next day she ran to see if the wind had blown it off, and to her delight it was still there. But the day after that she came back crying.

'What's the matter, Liesel?' I asked. 'Has the wind stolen the pink ribbon after all?'

'Oh, Nanny,' she sobbed, 'it's worse than that. The ribbon is gone, and the little tree too. Somebody has cut it down.'

I could hardly comfort her, and while I was trying to, her father, the tall Forester, came into the room with a pleasant-faced young fellow whom I knew to be the son of Peter

Gimsel, the chief peasant in the valley below us. Peter Gimsel was a rich man, and was now building himself a fine new chalet, which he intended one day for his son, Hans, when the boy was a few years older and got married. Hans had come up to tell the Forester that tomorrow they were going to put the roof on the chalet, and that the work would stop for a while while his father gave a big feast to all the workmen, and to his friends. For that was the custom in Switzerland, and it still is, whenever a house is being built. As the roof goes on, the work rests, the workmen eat, drink and make merry, and the householder's friends come to bless and wish happiness to the life that will be led under the roof. It is called the Roof-raising Feast.

This Hans was a nice lad, and when he saw Liesel crying, he stooped and smiled at her, and said, 'Don't cry, now, little one. Wouldn't you like to come to the party?'

'Oh, come, the child's too young,' said the Forester; 'you don't want to be bothered with children.'

But Liesel's face had cleared its clouds under the sunny smile of Hans, and he insisted. 'Yes, Forester, we want everybody, children and old folk too. So you'll come, Nanny, won't you?'

I said I would, and would bring Liesel with me, and take her home if the party went on past her bedtime; which it was very likely to do.

The next day we all put on our best; the Forester had his green suit with leather bindings, and an eagle's feather in his cap; I had on a dark-red stuff dress with a gaily coloured kerchief round my shoulders, and a black silk apron tied round my waist. And Liesel looked a picture in her fine white tucked chemise, her little blue skirt and black velvet bodice, and the tinkling silver chains that dangled from the embroidered collar round her neck. So, feeling very grand, we all went down to the valley, where there was already a great gathering of people about the new house; long tables, spread with good food, were set inside and outside, the fiddler was scraping away, and folk were talking, laughing, dancing, eating and casting away all care. As we approached, big Peter Gimsel got up from a table and shouted, 'Welcome, Forester, welcome!' And young Hans came running forward and took Liesel's hand and said, 'Welcome, little one! Look up there – we've just put up the Roof-tree!' For you must know that when the new roof goes on, it is the custom to set a little tree at the very top of the gable, as a sign that the house will grow in prosperity and happiness. Liesel's eyes followed where Hans was pointing, and there, on the top of the roof, as carefree as a child in the sunshine, was her own little fir tree, with the perky pink bow on the very tip-top.

'Oh, Nanny!' she cried. 'It is Liesel's tree.'

'Your tree, Liesel?' said Hans; and I told him what she meant. He laughed aloud and said, 'You must forgive me for stealing your tree for my house, little one. But it is your own fault, you know. When I went up to the forest to cut one, how could I help seeing the prettiest tree of all, when you had dressed it up in your own pink ribbon? That was the very reason why I cut it down. I thought the fairies had had a hand in it. Will you forgive me?'

Liesel blushed and smiled and said, 'Yes. I hope Liesel's tree will make your house very happy always, Master Hans.'

And so it did. For six years later, when Liesel was sixteen and Hans twenty-two, he brought her home to his house as his bride. And on the day of the wedding she wore in her hair the very pink bow she had tied on the little tree. For Hans had taken it off and kept it in his pocket for six years.

9. You Can't Darn *That* Hole

'WELL, well!' said the Old Nurse, putting her fist through the knee-cap of somebody's stocking. 'That's a hole and a half to be sure! Looks almost as if it were done a-purpose.'

'No, Nanny, I didn't, really!' cried Roley earnestly.

'And if you had done,' said the Old Nurse, 'I once knew a very great king who did likewise.'

'Were you his nurse, Nanny?' asked Doris.

'At one time; but he made the knee-hole I'm talking of when he was a hoary old man. Ah, well!' – the Old Nurse drew the stocking-leg over her hand – 'Where there's a hole, a darn can follow.'

'Was there ever a hole you couldn't darn, Nanny?' asked Doris.

'Only one that I can put a mind to.'

'What country was *that* in?' asked Ronnie.

'No country at all, in a manner of speaking. It was on the sea,' said the Old Nurse, 'where I happened to be sailing on a Norwegian merchantman, as nurse to Astrid, the Skipper's daughter.'

'Did you darn all the Norwegian sailors' socks, Nanny?' asked Roley.

'The Norwegian sailors had no socks to darn. But I darned the Skipper's socks, and he seemed to think I was one of the Seven Wonders of the World. And he thought his little daughter was the other six. Whatever she wanted, Olaf let her have. Fair spoiled her, as I often told him.'

*

Well, it happened one day that the Mate came along with a very grave face.

'Something serious to report, Skipper,' says he.

'Report away,' says the Skipper.

'It's something we found in the bilge,' says the Mate.

'A whale?' asks the Skipper.

'Not exactly,' says the Mate.

'A shrimp?' says the Skipper.

'Wrong again,' says the Mate.

'Speak up, man,' says the Skipper, 'and let's hear what you *did* find.'

'This is it,' says the Mate, and holds out on the palm of his hand a beautiful little baby, as transparent as a jellyfish, but not so floppy. It squirmed like a sand eel, and let out a sound like the high note of a singing shell.

The Skipper scratched his head. 'This looks more like your job than mine, Nanny,' he said. 'What do you advise?'

'Throw it back,' I told him. 'Believe me, there'll be trouble if you don't.'

At that moment up came little Astrid, and as she peered into the cradle of the Mate's brown hand, she cried, 'Let me look! Oh, the pretty little thing! You must not throw it back, Father; I want to keep it.'

'There'll be trouble,' I warned him again. But as I said before, Olaf could refuse his daughter nothing; and he said, 'Don't fuss, Nanny; let the child have her way.'

That night a big storm blew up out of nowhere. There hadn't been a sign of it on sea or sky for twenty-four hours ahead; yet the lightning flashed, the thunder crashed, the rainfall splashed, and the big waves dashed all over the tossing ship. It looked as though at any moment she must go to pieces. In the very height of the storm, a bearded figure rose up out of the tallest wave, and roared as loud as a thousand lions in one:

'Give back my baby, or I'll sink the ship!'

'What did I tell you?' I said to the Skipper. 'You've stolen Old King Neptune's child, and here he comes after you.' For I knew King Neptune well, and he knew me. So I nodded pleasantly to him for old time's sake, and said, 'Come, come, if you sink the ship you'll sink me too.'

'What, are you there, Nanny?' says Old King Neptune.

'There I am,' said I.

'Still darning, I see,' said he, 'and as well as ever.'

'There's nothing she can't darn,' said the Skipper.

'I wonder,' said Old Neptune.

'I'll go bail for it,' said the Skipper.

'Never mind my darning,' I told them; 'simmer down and talk business.'

Old Neptune calmed the waves while Astrid was sent for. She came, carrying the baby like the treasure of her heart, and when she heard she must give it up she burst into tears and said, 'I won't!'

'Then the ship will go down, darling,' I said.

'Let it!' cried Astrid. 'I won't!'

'And we'll all be drowned,' said the Mate.

'I don't care – I *won't*!' stormed Astrid. And so upset was she that her great fool of a father shook his fist in Neptune's face and said, 'She shan't! Do your worst!'

Neptune scratched his chin, and looked from Astrid to the Skipper, and from the Skipper to me.

'Hark ye, friend Olaf, I'll drive a bargain with you,' he said. 'You went bail just now that there was nothing old Nanny here couldn't darn.'

'I'll lay to that,' said the Skipper.

'Well, then, I say I can make a hole that's one too many for her.'

'I say you can't.'

'I say I can.'

'By Odin and Thor!' cried Olaf. 'If you can do that, you shall have your brat back, let mine squall as she pleases.' He winked at me, for such was his faith in me that he was sure the day was saved. And Old Neptune also winked, and I wondered what he had up his sleeve. For well he knew the skill of my needle.

Suddenly he sinks out of sight under the water, and a moment later thrusts his gigantic knee up through the sea again; and when he drew it back, there was the sucking whirlpool which today men call the Maelstrom, in the

75

very place where his knee had made the hole. The ship and all would have been sucked into it straightaway, if with his enormous hand Neptune had not pushed it out of danger. At the same moment, his dripping head appeared over the ship's side, and he said,

'There you are, Nanny! Darn *that* hole!'

'Take me to it, then,' I bade him, and he bore me on his shoulder to the brim of the whirlpool, where I threaded my needle at a flying jet of brine.

But could I draw it across the hole from edge to edge? Not I! No sooner was the first thread laid than it was whirled away into the vortex; and at last I patted old Neptune's top-knot (which I'd water-curled many a time in his babyhood), and said, 'Well, boy, you've beaten your Nanny for once.'

So he took me back to the ship, where the Skipper looked very glum at me, and handed the baby over. And before Astrid could blow up a squall, Old Neptune laid in

her lap the deep shell of an oyster, and in it was curled the loveliest little pearl baby you can possibly imagine. So *she* was satisfied, and Neptune was satisfied, and the ship was saved. But Olaf never thought quite so highly of me afterwards.

'There!' said the Old Nurse, biting off her thread, and holding Roley's stocking up; 'it was a bad hole, right enough – but it was easier to darn than the one King Neptune made when he put his kneecap through the sea.'

10. The Princess of China

'HERE'S a tiny hole, then!' said the Old Nurse, picking out Mary Matilda's little sock. 'Just a speck in the toe, and nothing more. But what would you expect of a baby, with a foot no bigger than that of the Princess of China?'

I was nurse to the Princess of China before England was old enough to know it had a name. I had been nurse before that to her mother, the Queen, who was now a widow. The Princess was the tiniest and most enchanting little creature in the world – as light as a butterfly, and as fragile as glass. A silver spoonful of rice made a big meal for her, and when she said, 'Oh, Nanny, I *am* so thirsty!' I would fill my thimble with milk and give it to her to drink; and then she left half of it. I made up her bed in my workbox, and cut my pocket handkerchief in two for a pair of sheets. Her laugh was like the tinkle of a raindrop falling on a glass bell. Really, when I went out walking I was afraid of losing her! So I slipped her into my purse, and left it open, and carried her like that. And as we walked through the streets of Peking, she would peep out of the purse and say, 'What a lot of big people there are in the world, Nanny!' But when we walked in the rice fields, and she saw the butterflies at play, she cried, 'Oh, Nanny! who are all those darling little people, and why do they never come to see me in the palace?'

One day a message came to the Queen of China that the Emperor of Tartary was coming to marry her daughter; and when the Princess had been told the news, she never stopped asking me a string of little questions. 'Where is Tartary, Nanny? Will I like Tartary? Are the people little there, or big? What is the Emperor like? Will I like him? Is he very enormous? Is he nice and tiny? What will he wear?'

I couldn't answer most of her questions, but when she came to the last one, I said, 'He'll wear purple, pet, like every other emperor.'

'Purple!' said she. 'How pretty! Now I shall know him when I see him, my pretty little Purple Emperor!' And the Princess of China clapped her tiny hands.

She grew very excited about her Purple Emperor, and the day he was expected she said suddenly, 'Nanny, I must have a new dress!'

'Why, poppet, you have seven hundred new dresses,' I told her, for hadn't I been kept busy sewing the tiny garments ever since the news came?

'I don't mean *those*,' said she, stamping her foot on my thumbnail, where she was standing at the time. 'I mean a dress that is *really* beautiful enough for a Purple Emperor.'

'Where shall we find it?' I asked her.

'We'll look for it in the rice fields,' said she. So I popped her into my purse, and we set out. The rice fields were as hot as ever, and as full of butterflies, and in them, besides ourselves, was a little Chinese boy, in a blue cotton shirt, chasing the butterflies. Just as we came up, he clapped his two hands together over such a little beauty, as delicate and pretty as a flower,

and when he parted his hands, the pretty thing fell dead at our feet. The Princess of China wept with rage.

'Make the boy stand still while I pull his hair!' she cried. And the boy had to come close and bend down his head, and she took hold of two of his hairs and pulled them as hard as she could, while he blinked his eyes a little. '*There!*' said she. 'Now go away. I'm never going to look at you again.'

When the boy had gone, the Princess of China said to me, 'Give me the poor little lady, Nanny.' So I picked up the butterfly and gave it to her, and she fondled its soft bloomy wings, and cried a little, and cuddled down inside the purse with it, so deep that I couldn't see her.

'Best let her get over her little fit by herself,' I thought; and looked about for a bit of shade to sit in till she was happy again. And there I rested, watching the butterflies dancing in the heat haze beyond the shadow; and especially one big fine fellow, the handsomest butterfly I had ever seen, who kept hovering in and out of the shadow, as though he couldn't keep away from us. At last, as I sat very still, he settled on my purse, and remained there quite a long while, moving his long slender feelers this way and that; so that I imagined he was saying something, if only I'd had ears tiny enough to hear him.

Whether I dozed or not, who can say? Perhaps I only nodded for a second or so. But when I next looked, I saw the handsome butterfly just spreading his wings to fly, and beside him was another butterfly, much smaller, and of the same pretty, delicate sort that the boy had killed. They rose together, their wings touching, and flew out into the sunshine, where they danced awhile, and then disappeared in the haze.

I thought it was now time to return, in case the Emperor of Tartary should be arriving, so I called into my purse, 'Come, poppet, we're going home!' There was no answer, and I supposed she was asleep; so I got up and walked home quietly, not to wake her.

When I reached the palace, the Queen ran out to meet me in a fluster. 'Oh, there you are, Nanny!' said she. 'The Emperor is just entering the city, and we couldn't find you or the Princess anywhere.'

'Here she is, safe in my purse,' I said; and we opened the purse, and it was as empty as an air-balloon. We searched every corner of it in vain, and then we ran back together to the rice fields, looking for her in the dust on the way, though I knew she could not have fallen out as I came home without my seeing it. When we came to the shadow where I had been sitting, we searched the ground thoroughly, but there was not a sign of her. There was nothing but the two butterflies, who had come back, and settled first upon my hand, and then upon the Queen's. And the little pretty one fluttered her wings at me, as

though to say, 'See my lovely new dress!' Then it struck me, all of a sudden, and I said to the Queen, who was weeping, 'What sort of a butterfly is this?'

'What a time to ask, Nanny!' wailed the Queen. 'I don't know what sort it is. The big one's a Purple Emperor. But what a time to ask!'

'Dry your eyes,' I said. 'It's useless to look any more. The Princess of China is gone where she'll never come back from.' And I shook the two butterflies off my hand, and led the Queen home.

We were met at the palace gates by an excited crowd. The Emperor of Tartary had arrived, and there was no bride to greet him. But as we appeared, the crowd cried, 'Here they are! Here's the Princess's Nurse!' and down the steps strode the Emperor of Tartary himself, a great big handsome man, in a royal purple mantle. He came straight to the Queen and hugged her, saying, 'My Princess! My Bride! My Beautiful One!'

It took the Queen's breath away, and ours too. But as soon as she could, she made a sign to me to say nothing, and while the Emperor embraced her again I signed to the crowd. They all understood, and folded their hands in their sleeves, and stood with downcast eyes as the Emperor of Tartary led his bride into the palace. And where was the harm of it? What would he have done with my tiny Princess of China for a bride? He was much better off as he was.

*

'I thought it was going to be a tinier tale than that, Nanny,' said Doris, 'because the hole in Mary Matilda's sock was so tiny.'

'Ah,' said the Old Nurse, 'but tiny holes take very fine darning.'

11. The Golden Eagle

'HOWEVER you boys manage to get these holes in your stocking-knees,' said the Old Nurse, taking a pair of stockings out of her basket, 'I really can't think! You've been climbing trees again, *I* know! Just like Lionello, who climbed his father's olive tree to catch a golden eagle.'

'Who was Lionello, Nanny?' asked Roley. 'Is he a big enough story to go into that hole?' He hoped Lionello *was*, for then he would be a very long story indeed. The Old Nurse had just put the whole of her fist through the hole in his stocking-knee.

'Yes,' said she, 'Lionello will just about fit this hole.' And having threaded her darning needle, she began.

Lionello lived in Italy, and his father was the gardener to the big house where I was then staying as nurse. So, though I was not Lionello's nurse, I knew all about him, and saw him every day. He was a very carefree, happy sort of boy, and rather fond of boasting. The master of the house was a count, and the gardens were splendid; but the Count himself was a quiet little man, and slipped about the place like a shadow, while Master Lionello strutted up and down between the roses and the fig trees, the statues and the fountains, as though he owned the place. And often I heard him speak to his little friends, the children of the peasants round about, in some such words as these:

'You ought to see *our* garden! In *our* garden the figs are as big as melons, and each rose is as big as a whole bouquet! In *our* garden the fountains aren't filled with water, but with champagne! In *our* garden, the statues are so fine, that the King of Italy has none so beautiful! In *our* garden, this, that, and the other thing!' – I couldn't tell you all the wonders Lionello invented about the garden that didn't belong to him.

Well, that's by the way, just to show you the sort of boy he was.

One day I met him at the foot of the garden, where his father's cottage was, and the little bit of land that the Count let him have for himself. Lionello had a net in his hand, and was prancing along looking very bold and daring.

'Well, Lionello,' I said, 'you look as though you were going to meet a dragon.'

'Oh, no,' he said carelessly, 'I'm just going to catch a golden eagle.'

'Indeed,' said I, 'and where will you find one?'

'In my father's olive tree,' said Lionello. 'That's where they always are.'

Off he went, and I followed him to see what happened. Soon I heard a great squawking from the top of one of the trees, and a flurry of wings and feathers, and Lionello's voice shouting – all the noises were mixed up together, so that a great adventure seemed to be afoot. By the time I reached the tree, Lionello was coming down it, with his shirt torn, and a great hole in his stocking, a scratch on his cheek, and his mother's old yellow hen under his arm. We met at the bottom of the tree, and I said, 'Well, Lionello, so you caught your golden eagle, then?'

'Yes,' he said carelessly, 'there she goes!' And he tossed the hen from him, as much as to say, 'Really, we have so many golden eagles about, they're hardly worth keeping.' Well, that's by the way, but it shows you the sort of boy Lionello was.

Before Lionello grew up, I left the Count to go to be a nurse to the children of a Cannibal King for a while; but a few years later I happened to be in that part of Italy again, and went to see the children of the Count, for I never forget any of the boys and girls I've nursed. The Count's children were grown up now, and the son of the house was about to be married to the most beautiful girl in the neighbourhood. His young bride was there; I had remembered her as a lovely little girl, and kissed her and approved of her. Then I said, 'By the way, what has happened to Lionello?'

'He is still in the same cottage,' smiled the Count's son, 'and he is our gardener now, for his father is dead. Lionello got married last week.'

'Really,' I said. 'And whom did he marry?'

'He married the charcoal-seller's daughter, Anita.'

'I remember,' I said; 'a nice little girl with a big mouth and a turned-up nose!'

When I had taken leave of the happy young couple, I went down through the gardens to find Lionello. He was watering the roses at the foot of the terrace, and called out gaily to me from a distance.

'Olà, Nanny! How glad I am to see you again.'

'I'm glad to see you too, Lionello, and glad you have not forgotten me.'

'As if I could forget you!' laughed the handsome young fellow. 'You haven't changed a bit.'

'And I don't think you have either, Lionello,' I said, for though of course he was taller and bigger, he had the same gay air and bright dark eyes as when he was a boy. But at my words he laughed, and said, 'Not changed, Nanny? Haven't I, though! I hope I have. Do you remember how I used to deceive myself when I was a little boy? Why, I used to think my mother's old yellow hen was a golden eagle. Ha, ha, ha! Don't you remember that? I thought I was taking you all in, and all the time I was only taking myself in.'

'Well, it kept you happy,' I said.

'Oh, yes, I was happy enough; and in that, at least, I'm not changed. I'm happier than ever now!' He looked at me, smiled, and said gaily, 'I got married last week.'

'Did you, Lionello?'

'Yes, it's true; and whom do you think I've married, Nanny? Why, the most beautiful girl in Italy.'

'Really, Lionello?'

'Really, Nanny! I'll tell you a funny thing. The young Count up at the house is getting married too; but he couldn't make up his mind to, until I'd married Anita. Then, all of a sudden, as though he knew he'd missed the best, he took the next best; and a charming girl she is – but not like Anita. You must come along and see her now.'

I walked down to the old cottage with Lionello, wondering how time had turned the plain little Anita into such a beauty. She came out of the cottage as we approached, and ran

to greet me, smiling very sweetly at me, and more sweetly still at Lionello.

The smile so brightened her face, that it didn't matter that she had grown up plainer than ever, and that her nose still turned up. And Lionello beamed upon her, and whispered in my ear, 'There, Nanny, what did I tell you? The most beautiful girl in Italy!'

'Oh, Nanny,' cried Roley, as the Old Nurse cut off the thread, 'the tale can't be done by now! The hole was *much* bigger than that.'

'Yes, it looked like it,' said the Old Nurse, 'but some holes, my dear, are so big, that they can only be cobbled.'

12. The Two Brothers

'AH!' SAID the Old Nurse, shaking her head over the heap of undarned stockings in her basket, 'the boys and girls in Greece once wore no stockings, and very glad their mothers would have been, if they could have known what they'd been spared.'

'Couldn't you tell them, Nanny?' asked Doris.

'I didn't know myself, my dear, at that time, when I was nurse to the little Thalia' (the Old Nurse said Thalia to rhyme with Maria). 'Nobody had begun to think of stockings then. Thalia had but one garment to wear – a

97

little white tunic, that left her arms and legs and neck bare. Her only other adornment was a girdle of green leaves, which she would weave for herself in the woods, and a wreath of flowers, which she plucked in the meadows. She was the only daughter of the Duke of Athens, and she had two brothers, ten years older than herself, who were twins like Ronnie and Roley. Only they were much older than Ronnie and Roley are; they were twenty years old when Thalia was ten.'

The names of these brothers were Cymon and Damon, and they were both so fond of their little sister that they were jealous of each other, though they had loved each other dearly as boys. But when their baby sister was no longer a baby, and had grown into a charming little girl, Damon and Cymon vied with each other as to which could please her best, and win her tenderest signs of affection. And the day she seemed to prefer Cymon, Damon was dark and unhappy; and the day she clung most to Damon, Cymon drew apart, and would not speak to his brother.

One day Thalia disappeared. She had run out of the palace when I was not looking, but this she often did, so at first we were not much alarmed. But when she had been missing for a few hours, we started to search for her in good earnest, and soon it was plain that she was not in the palace, or in the city either. The Duke sent messengers into every quarter of Athens, where everybody knew and was proud of the little Thalia. They would not have harmed a hair of her head. But no one had seen her. So then we began to search outside the city, and at last on the mountain we found an old shepherd carrying a lamb back to the fold. We asked him if he had seen a child that day, and he answered,

'Yes. A little girl came my way this morning, and stayed to play with my young lambs. I did not know who she was, but the lambs were not afraid of her, so I let her stay. After a while, I saw the shadow of wings passing overhead. I feared it might be an eagle, come to swoop down on my flock, and hastened to gather them in. But then I saw it was no eagle, but the bright figure of a god on winged feet, who flew down to earth and gathered up, not my lambs, but the little girl you are seeking.'

We knew by the old man's tale that our little Thalia had been stolen by Hermes, who alone among the gods has wings on his feet. Damon cried out, 'I will find my sister or die!' And at the same moment Cymon cried, 'I will not live unless I find Thalia!'

'Are you her brothers?' asked the old shepherd.

'Yes,' they answered together.

'Then,' said the shepherd, 'I have a message for you. When he was some twenty foot in air above my head, Hermes stopped and called to me: "When the two brothers of this child come seeking her, tell them that I will restore her to the one who will give up most for her. And let them say in your hearing what they are ready to give up, for, invisible though I shall be, I will be near to hear them." '

'O Hermes!' cried Damon. 'Wherever you may be, listening to me now, restore my sister to me, and I will give up my strength, even though it means that I shall never be able to touch her soft cheek again.'

'O Hermes!' cried Cymon. 'I will give up not only my strength, but also my speech, so that I may not even speak her name to her.'

'O Hermes!' said Damon. 'I will give up not only my strength and my speech, but my sight, so that I can neither touch her, nor call to her, nor see her.'

'O Hermes!' cried Cymon. 'I will give up my strength, my speech, my sight, and also my hearing, so that I cannot touch or see her, or call her, or hear her call me.'

'As well as all this,' then said Damon, 'I will give up my life if Thalia is safe restored.'

'And I, too, Hermes,' cried Cymon eagerly; 'I, too, will gladly die to save my sister.'

And he and Damon glared at one another, each fearful lest his brother should give up something he had not thought of. And it seemed to both of them that when they had given up their lives, they had given up all they could. So they waited, hoping to see their sister once again before they died.

But nothing happened. The god did not appear, and their sister seemed lost for ever. Then at the same instant tears sprang into their eyes, the look of hate in them was softened by sorrow, and the brothers held out their hands to one another. And they said, in the same breath, in the same words,

'Brother, our sister is lost to us both; but if only she could be restored to us I would give up my jealousy for ever, and give her to you gladly.'

Even as they said these words, the old shepherd breathed thrice upon the lamb in his arms, and there stood the little Thalia once more, as lovely and laughing as ever. And as she ran into the arms of her two brothers, the shepherd's age fell from him; before their eyes he took the shape of a glorious youth with wings upon his feet, and he rose up into the air like a bright bird, and vanished out of sight.

13. The Sea-Baby

THE STOCKING-BASKET was empty. For once there was nothing to darn. The Old Nurse had told so many stories that she had mended all the holes made by Doris and Mary Matilda, and even by Ronnie and Roley. Tomorrow they would make some more, of course, but tonight the Old Nurse sat with her hands folded in her lap, and watched the children fall asleep by firelight.

Only one of them kept awake. Mary Matilda would not go to sleep. She was not cross, she was not ill, there was no reason at all except that she was wide awake. She kept on standing up in her cot and laughing at the Old Nurse over the bars. And when the Old Nurse came and laid her down and tucked her up, she turned over and laughed at the old Nurse *between* the cot bars.

'Go to sleep, Mary Matilda,' said the Old Nurse in her hush-hush voice. 'Shut your eyes, my darling, and go to sleep.'

But Mary Matilda couldn't, or if she could, she wouldn't. And at last the Old Nurse did what she very seldom did: she came over to Mary Matilda, and took her out of the cot, and carried her to the fire, and rocked her on her knee.

'Can't you go to sleep, baby?' she crooned. 'Can't you go to sleep, then? Ah, you're just my Sea-Baby over again! *She* never went to sleep, either, all the time I nursed her. And she was the very first I ever nursed. I've never told anybody about her since, but I'll tell you,

Mary Matilda. So shut your eyes and listen, while I tell about my Sea-Baby.'

I couldn't tell you when it happened: it was certainly a long time after the Flood, and I know I was only about ten years old, and had never left the Norfolk village on the sea coast where I was born. My father was a fisherman, and a tiller of the land; and my mother kept the house and spun the wool and linen for our clothes. But that tells us nothing, for fathers have provided the food, and mothers have kept the house, since the beginning of things. So don't go asking any more when it was that I nursed my very first baby.

It happened like this, Mary Matilda. Our cottage stood near the edge of the cliff, and at high tide the sea came right up to the foot, but at low tide it ran so far back that it seemed almost too far to follow it. People said that once, long ago, the sea had not come in so close; and that the cliff had gone out many miles farther. And on the far end of the cliff had stood another village. But after the Flood all that part of the cliff was drowned under the sea, and the village along with it. And there, said the people, the village still lay, far out to sea under the waves; and on stormy nights, they said, you could hear the church bells ringing in the church tower below the water. Ah, don't you start laughing at your old Nanny now! We knew it was true, I tell you. And one day something happened to prove it.

A big storm blew up over our part of the land; the biggest storm that any of us could remember, so big that we thought the Flood had come again. The sky was as black as night all day long, and the wind blew so hard that it drove a strong man backwards, and the rain poured down so that you only had to hold a pitcher out of the window for a second, and when you took it in it was flowing over, and the thunder growled and crackled so that we had to make signs to each other, for talking was no use, and the lightning flashed so bright that my mother could thread her needle by it. That *was* a storm, that was! My mother was frightened, but my father, who was weather-wise, watched the sky and said from time to time, 'I think that'll come out all right.' And so it did. The lightning and thunder flashed and rolled themselves away into the distance, the rain stopped, the wind died down, the sky cleared up for a beautiful evening, and the sun turned all the vast wet sands to a sheet of gold as far as the eye could see. Yes, and farther! For a wonder had happened during the storm. The sea had been driven back so far that it had vanished out of sight, and sands were laid bare that no living man or woman had viewed before. And there, far, far across the golden beach, lay a tiny village, shining in the setting sun.

Think of our excitement, Mary Matilda! It was the drowned village of long ago, come back to the light of day.

Everybody gathered on the shore to look at it. And suddenly I began to run towards it, and all the other children followed me. At first our parents called, 'Come back! Come back! The sea may come rolling in before you can get there.' But we were too eager to see the village for ourselves, and in the end the big folk felt the same about it; and they came running after the children across the sands. As we drew nearer, the little houses became plainer, looking like blocks of gold in the evening light; and the little streets appeared like golden brooks, and the church spire in the middle was like a point of fire.

For all my little legs, I was the first to reach the village. I had had a start of the others, and could always run fast as a child and never tire. We had long stopped running, of course, for the village was so far out that our breath would not last. But I was still walking rapidly when I reached the village and turned a corner. As I did so, I heard one of the big folk cry,

'Oh, look! Yonder lies the sea.' I glanced ahead, and did see, on the far horizon beyond the village, the shining line of the sea that had gone so far away. Then I heard another grown-up cry, 'Take care! Take care! Who knows when it may begin to roll back again? We have come far, and oh, suppose the sea should overtake us before we can reach home!' Then, peeping round my corner, I saw everybody take fright and turn tail, running as hard as they could across the mile or so of sands they had just crossed. But nobody had noticed me, or thought of me; no doubt my own parents thought I was one of the band of running children, and so they left me alone there, with all the little village to myself.

What a lovely time I had, going into the houses, up and down the streets, and through the church. Everything was left as it had been, and seemed ready for someone to come to; the flowers were blooming in the gardens, the fruit was hanging on the trees, the tables were spread for the next meal, a pot was standing by the kettle on the hearth in one house, and in another there were toys upon the floor. And when I began to go upstairs to the other rooms, I found in every bed someone asleep. Grandmothers and grandfathers, mothers and fathers, young men and young women, boys and girls: all so fast asleep that there was no waking them. And at last, in a little room at the top of a house, I found a baby in a cradle, wide awake.

She was the sweetest baby I had ever seen. Her eyes were as blue as the sea that had covered them so long, her skin as white as the foam, and her little round head as gold as the sands in the evening sunlight. When she saw me, she sat up in her cradle, and crowed with delight. I knelt down beside her, held out my arms, and she cuddled into them with a little gleeful chuckle. I carried her about the room, dancing her up and down in my arms, calling her my baby, my pretty Sea-Baby, and showing her the things in the room and out of the window. But as we were looking out of the window at a bird's nest in a tree, I seemed to see the shining line of water on the horizon begin to move.

'The sea is coming in!' I thought. 'I must hurry back before it catches us.' And I flew out of the house with the Sea-Baby in my arms, and ran as fast as I could out of the village, and followed the crowd of golden footsteps on the sands, anxious to get home soon. When I had to pause to get my breath, I ventured to glance over my shoulder, and there behind me lay the little village, still glinting in the sun. On I ran again, and after a while was forced to stop a second time. Once more I glanced behind me, and this time the village was not to be seen: it had disappeared beneath the tide of the sea, which was rolling in behind me.

Then how I scampered over the rest of the way! I reached home just as the tiny wavelets, which run in front of the big waves, began to lap my ankles, and I scrambled up the cliff, with the Sea-Baby in my arms, and got indoors, panting for breath. Nobody was at home, for as it happened they were all out looking for me. So I took my baby upstairs, and put her to bed in my own bed, and got her some warm milk. But she turned from the milk, and wouldn't drink it. She only seemed to want to laugh and play with me. So I did for a little while, and then I told her she must go to sleep. But she only laughed some more, and went on playing.

'Shut your eyes, baby,' I said to her, 'hush-hush! Hush-hush!' (just as my own mother said to me). But the baby didn't seem to understand, and went on laughing.

Then I said, 'You're a very naughty baby' (as my mother sometimes used to say to me). But she didn't mind that either, and just went on laughing. So in the end I had to laugh too, and play with her.

My mother heard us, when she came into the house; and she ran up to find me, delighted that I was safe. What was her surprise to find the baby with me! She asked me where it had come from, and I told her; and she called my father, and he stood scratching his head, as most men do when they aren't quite sure about a thing.

'I want to keep it for my own, Mother,' I said.

'Well, we can't turn it out now it's in,' said my mother. 'But you'll have to look after it yourself, mind.'

I wanted nothing better! I'd always wanted to nurse things, whether it was a log of wood, or a kitten, or my mother's shawl rolled into a dumpy bundle. And now I had a little live baby of my own to nurse. How I did enjoy myself that week! I did everything for it; dressed and undressed it, washed it, and combed its hair; and played and danced with it, and talked with it and walked with it. And I tried to give it its meals, but it wouldn't eat; and I tried to put it to sleep, but it wouldn't shut its eyes. No, not for anything I could do, though I sang to it, and rocked it, and told it little stories.

It didn't worry me much, for I knew no better: but it worried my mother, and I heard her say to my father, 'There's something queer about that child. I don't know, I'm sure!'

On the seventh night after the storm, I woke up suddenly from my dreams, as I lay in bed with my baby beside me. It was very late, my parents had long gone to bed themselves, and what had wakened me I did not know, for I heard no sound at all. The moon was very bright, and filled the square of my windowpane with silver light; and through the air outside I saw something swimming – I thought at first it was a white cloud, but as it reached my open window I saw it was a lady, moving along the air as though she were swimming in water. And the strange thing was that her eyes were fast shut; so that as her white arms moved out and in she seemed to be swimming not only in the air, but in her sleep.

She swam straight through my open window to the bedside, and there she came to rest, letting her feet down upon the floor like a swimmer setting his feet on the sands under his body. The lady leaned over the bed with her shut eyes, and took my wide-awake baby in her arms.

'*Hush-hush! Hush-hush!*' she said; and the sound of her voice was not like my mother's voice when she said it, but like the waves washing the shore on a still night; such a

peaceful sound, the sort of sound that might have been the first sound made in the world, or else the last. You couldn't help wanting to sleep as you heard her say it. I felt my head begin to nod, and as it grew heavier and heavier, I noticed that my Sea-Baby's eyelids were beginning to droop too. Before I could see any more, I fell asleep; and when I awoke in the morning my baby had gone.

*

'Where to, Mary Matilda? Ah, you mustn't ask me that! I only know she must have gone where all babies go when they go to sleep. Go to sleep. Hush-hush! *Hush-hush! Go to sleep!*'

Mary Matilda had gone to sleep at last. The Old Nurse laid her softly in her cot, turned down the light, and crept out of the nursery.

Extra!

Extra!

READ ALL ABOUT IT!

ELEANOR FARJEON

THE OLD NURSE'S
STOCKING-BASKET

ELEANOR FARJEON

THE OLD NURSE'S STOCKING-BASKET

Illustrated by Edward Ardizzone

A PUFFIN BOOK

1881	*Eleanor is born* on 13 February in London
1886	*Eleanor is home-schooled and spends hours in her attic reading*
1899	*Eleanor writes the libretto for her older brother, Harry's, operetta entitled* Floretta. *The operetta goes on to be produced by the Royal Academy of Music*
1914	*Eleanor becomes a regular writer for* The Daily Herald, *as well as other newspapers, and magazines like* Punch
1916	*One of Eleanor's most popular works,* Nursery Rhymes of London Town, *is published*
1931	*She writes the hymn* Morning Has Broken, *which is still very popular today. Her work* The Old Nurse's Stocking-Basket *is published*

1935	A Nursery in the Nineties, *the autobiography of Eleanor's childhood is published*
1955	*Eleanor wins the highly prestigious Carnegie Medal for* The Little Bookroom
1956	*Eleanor is awarded the Hans Christian Andersen International Medal for her contribution to children's literature across her career*
1959	*Eleanor is the first recipient of the American Catholic Library Association's Regina Medal, for distinguished contribution to children's literature*
1965	*Eleanor dies on 5 June in London, aged eighty-four*

INTERESTING FACTS

Eleanor was known by her family as 'Nellie'.

Following her death, The Children's Book Circle (an organization run by volunteers from the publishing industry) created the Eleanor Farjeon Award, presented annually to individuals or companies that have made an outstanding contribution to Children's Literature. Previous winners include Jacqueline Wilson, Quentin Blake and the Polka Theatre.

ABOUT THE ILLUSTRATOR

EDWARD ARDIZZONE

Edward Ardizzone was an English artist and an award-winning writer and illustrator of children's books. During the Second World War, Edward was appointed Official War Artist and was even commissioned to paint a portrait of the Prime Minister, Winston Churchill! He illustrated many of Eleanor Farjeon's children's books, including The Little Book Room *and* The Eleanor Farjeon Book.

WHERE DID THE
STORY COME FROM?

*Eleanor came from a creative family
background. Her father, Ben Farjeon, was a
well-known Victorian novelist and her mother,
Maggie, was the daughter of the famous American
actor, Joseph Jefferson. Many of Eleanor's stories
were drawn from the imaginative games she played
with her brothers when they were all children.*

GUESS WHO?

A   *'Put back my heart and take away my temper'*

B   *'Give me back my baby, or I'll sink the ship'*

C   *'I am the proudest in all Castile'*

D   *'She was so beautiful she had to wear a veil over her face'*

E   *'In our garden the figs are as big as melons, and each rose is as big as a whole bouquet!'*

WORDS GLORIOUS WORDS!

Lots of *words* have several different meanings – here are a few you'll find in this Puffin book. Use a *dictionary* or look them up online to find other definitions.

Rhine *A European river stretching for 820 miles from Switzerland to the North Sea*

veil *a piece of material worn by women to cover the face*

quarrelling *arguing or disagreeing*

scamper *to move with quick, light steps*

bodice *the part of a woman's dress that is above the waist*

champagne *a white, sparkling wine from the region of Champagne in France*

QUIZ

1 *What does the Old Nanny do whilst she sits by the fire telling stories?*

a) *Darns stockings*
b) *Eats her dinner*
c) *Paints*
d) *Folds laundry*

2 *What part of the body did the Prince of India have removed by the Magician?*

a) *His legs*
b) *His heart*
c) *His brain*
d) *His hands*

3 Why does Lionello climb his father's olive tree?

a) Because he likes to climb trees

b) To pick olives

c) To get a good view of the gardens

d) To catch a golden eagle

4 What do the brothers Damon and Cymon give up in order for Thalia to be returned to them?

a) Their eyesight

b) Their jealousy

c) Chocolate and sweets

d) Their sense of smell

5 Where do the Rag-picker's Son and the little Duke go swimming?

a) In the river

b) In a large puddle

c) In a swimming pool

d) In the sea

ANSWERS: 1) b 2) a 3) d 4) b 5) a

IN
THIS YEAR

1931
Fact Pack

What else was
happening in the
world when this Puffin
book was published?

The *Empire State Building* officially opens in
New York.

The strongest **earthquake** in Great Britain ever
recorded occurs, measuring 6.1 on the *Richter* scale.

The **electric razor** is invented and goes on sale.

The first non-stop flight takes place across the Pacific
Ocean, from Japan, to America.

MAKE AND DO

Make bread like the Infanta of Spain!

Bread is yummy and simple to make. You might need an adult to help you.

YOU WILL NEED:

* 500g strong white flour, and some extra for when you're kneading the dough
* 2 tsp salt
* 300ml water
* a sachet of yeast
* 3 tbsp olive oil
* Large bowl
* Baking tray
* Oven
* Knife
* Wire rack

1. In a large bowl, mix the flour, salt and yeast.

2. Make a dip in the middle and pour in the water and oil. Mix everything together well.

3. Take the dough out and knead it with your knuckles on a lightly floured surface. When the dough is really smooth place it back into the bowl, cover with a damp tea towel and leave it for at least an hour. This is called proving.

4. Put the dough on a baking tray and leave to prove for another hour.

5. Preheat your oven to 220°C.

6. Dust the dough with flour and carefully, with a knife, cut a cross on the top.

7. Bake until the loaf sounds hollow when you tap its bottom and the top is nice and brown. Leave it to cool on a wire rack.

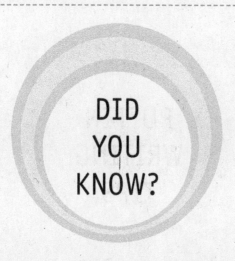

DID
YOU
KNOW?

Eleanor Farjeon published more than sixty books, most of which were for children.

Together with Herbert, her younger brother, she also wrote a children's pantomime, two operettas and a musical fairy story, The Glass Slipper, *based on the classic tale of Cinderella.*

Eleanor Farjeon was born in the same year as many famous people including the painter Pablo Picasso, the ballet dancer Anna Pavlova and scientist Alexander Fleming.

PUFFIN WRITING TIPS

On your marks, get set, GO! Set a stopwatch and see how much you can write in a minute.

Write a description of your hometown – as if you were talking to an alien.

Keep a travel journal when you go on holiday so you can capture all the exciting new sights and sounds.

A Puffin Book can take you to amazing places.

WHERE WILL YOU GO?

#PackAPuffin

stories that last a lifetime

Animal tales

- [ ] *The Trumpet of the Swan*
- [ ] *Gobbolino*
- [ ] *Tarka the Otter*
- [ ] *Watership Down*
- [ ] *A Dog So Small*

War stories

- [ ] *Goodnight Mister Tom*
- [ ] *Back Home*
- [ ] *Carrie's War*

Magical adventures

- [ ] *The Neverending Story*
- [ ] *Mrs Frisby and the Rats of NIMH*
- [ ] *A Wrinkle in Time*

Unusual friends

- [ ] *Stig of the Dump*
- [ ] *Stuart Little*
- [ ] *The Borrowers*
- [ ] *Charlotte's Web*
- [ ] *The Cay*

Real life

- [ ] *Roll of Thunder, Hear My Cry*
- [ ] *The Family from One End Street*
- [ ] *Annie*
- [ ] *Smith*

stories that last a lifetime

Ever wanted a friend who could take you to magical realms,
talk to animals or help you survive a shipwreck? Well, you'll find
them all in the **A PUFFIN BOOK** collection.

A PUFFIN BOOK will stay with you **forever**.
Maybe you'll read it again and again, or perhaps years from now
you'll suddenly **remember** the moment it made you **laugh** or
cry or simply see things **differently**. Adventurers **big** and **small**,
rebels out to **change** their world, even a mouse with a **dream**
and a spider who can spell – these are the characters who
make **stories** that last a **lifetime**.

Whether you love animal tales, war stories or want to
know what it was like growing up in a different time and place,
the **A PUFFIN BOOK** collection has a story for you
– you just need to decide where you want to go next . . .